The Boy who cried Wolf

Based on a story by Aesop

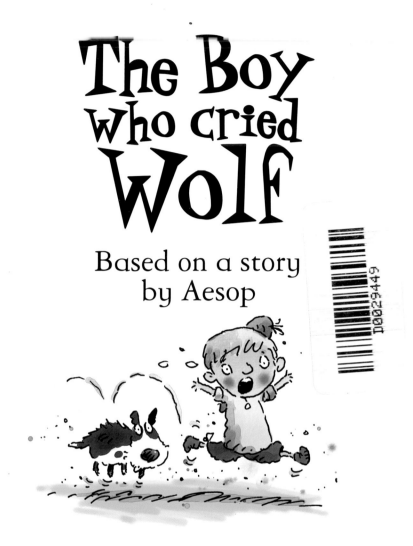

Retold by Mairi Mackinnon

Illustrated by
Mike and Carl Gordon

Reading Consultant: Alison Kelly
Roehampton University

This story is about

Sam,

some sheep,

the villagers

and (maybe) a wolf.

Sam lived in a little
village in the mountains.

Every day he took the
sheep from the village...

He watched them from
morning until evening.

Then he took them home
again.

Every day was the same.

Sam was lonely and he was SO bored.

All his friends were down
in the village.

11

Baa-aa.

But they didn't
have much to say.

13

"Nobody ever comes up here," moaned Sam.

"Nothing ever happens."

One day, he had an idea.

He ran down the hill to
the village.

"A wolf!" he shouted.
"A wolf has come out of
the forest!"

Everyone ran up the hill with him.

Puffing and panting, they reached the meadow.

Of course, there was no wolf.

The sheep were quietly
eating their grass.

The villagers were angry,
but Sam just laughed.

A few days later, Sam was bored again. He ran down the hill to the village.

"A wolf!" he shouted.
"A wolf has come out of
the forest!"

25

But most ran up the hill
to see.

Puffing and panting, they reached the meadow.

Of course, there was no wolf.

The sheep were quietly
eating their grass.

Everyone was very angry,
but Sam just laughed.

A week later, Sam was bored again. He ran down the hill to the village.

Most people didn't believe
him this time. Just a few
ran up the hill.

Puffing and panting, they reached the meadow.

Of course, there was no wolf.

The sheep were quietly
eating their grass.

Now everyone
was furious. Sam
laughed and laughed.

A few days later, a wolf
DID come out of the forest.

Sam was terrified. He ran down to the village as fast as he could.

Nobody believed him.

Sam begged them to
come with him.

This time, they just
laughed at him.

In the end, Sam had
to go back up the hill
all alone.

The wolf had killed some
of the sheep.

The rest had
run away.

Sam stayed in the meadow
until it was dark.

Finally, the villagers
came to find him.

"Why didn't you believe me?" he asked.

"You always told lies before," they said.

"I've learned my lesson. Never again," said Sam.

About this story

"The Boy who cried Wolf"
is one of Aesop's (say Ee-sop's)
Fables. These are a collection
of short stories, first told in
Ancient Greece around
4,000 years ago.

Nobody knows exactly who
Aesop was, but the stories
are still popular today, and
they are known all around
the world.

The stories are often about animals, and they always have a "moral" (a message or lesson) at the end.

The moral of the story about the boy who cried wolf is:

No one believes liars, even when they tell the truth.

Series editor: Lesley Sims

Designed by Michelle Lawrence

First published in 2008 by Usborne Publishing Ltd.,
83-85 Saffron Hill, London EC1N 8RT, England.
www.usborne.com
Copyright © 2008 Usborne Publishing Ltd.